were

The Red Sneakers

by Liza Charlesworth

ISBN: 978-1-338-78276-9
Illustrated by Kevin Zimmer
Copyright © 2021 by Liza Charlesworth. All rights reserved.
Published by Scholastic Inc., 557 Broadway, New York, NY 10012

10 9 8 7 6 5 4 3 2 1   68   21 22 23 24 25 26 27/0

Printed in Jiaxing, China. First printing, June 2021.

The red sneakers **were** walking in the woods. Walk, walk!

The red sneakers **were** walking in the grass. Walk, walk!

The red sneakers **were** walking in the flowers. Walk, walk!

The red sneakers **were** walking in the puddles. Walk, walk!

The red sneakers **were** walking in the house. Walk, walk!

The red sneakers **were**
talking to the girl.
Talk, talk!

The red sneakers **were** walking in the woods. Walk, walk!